HIGHER ON THE DOOR

by James Stevenson

Greenwillow Books, New York

The illustrations are watercolor. The text type is ITC Bookman Light.

Copyright © 1987 by James Stevenson All rights reserved.

Printed in Hong Kong by South China Printing Co. First Edition 10 9 8 7 6 5 4 3 2 1

Library of Congress Cataloging-in-Publication Data

Stevenson, James (date) Higher on the door.

Summary: James Stevenson remembers what it was like growing up in a village, sometimes taking the train to New York City, and waiting to get older.

1. Stevenson, James (date) —Biography—Youth— Juvenile literature. 2. Authors, American—20th century— Biography—Juvenile literature. 3. Illustrators—United States— Biography—Juvenile literature. [1. Stevenson, James (date). 2. Authors, American. 3. Illustrators]   I. Title. PS3569.T4557Z476 1987 741.64'2'0924 [92]   86-14925 ISBN 0-688-06636-4 ISBN 0-688-06637-2 (lib. bdg.)

I have a grandson now; that's
how old I am. But sometimes I
look back and remember . . .

Years ago, on our birthdays,
our mother marked on a doorway
how much we had grown.

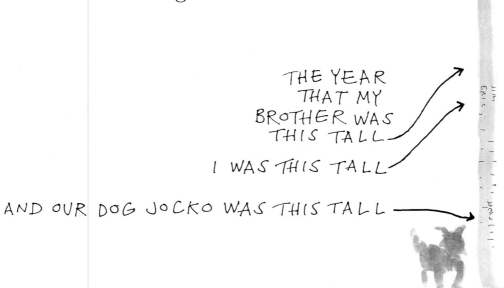

THE YEAR
THAT MY
BROTHER WAS
THIS TALL

I WAS THIS TALL

AND OUR DOG JOCKO WAS THIS TALL

We lived on a street in a village by the river.

CLINK
CLINK

DRIP
DRIP

On our street,
the milkman brought
milk in glass bottles, and
took away the empties.

The iceman brought
ice for our icebox,

and the coal truck came and sent coal thundering into our cellar.

We knew our neighbors pretty well.

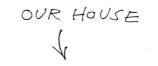

OUR HOUSE

↑
NICE

↑
NO
FUN

↑
NOT
NICE

↑
O.K.

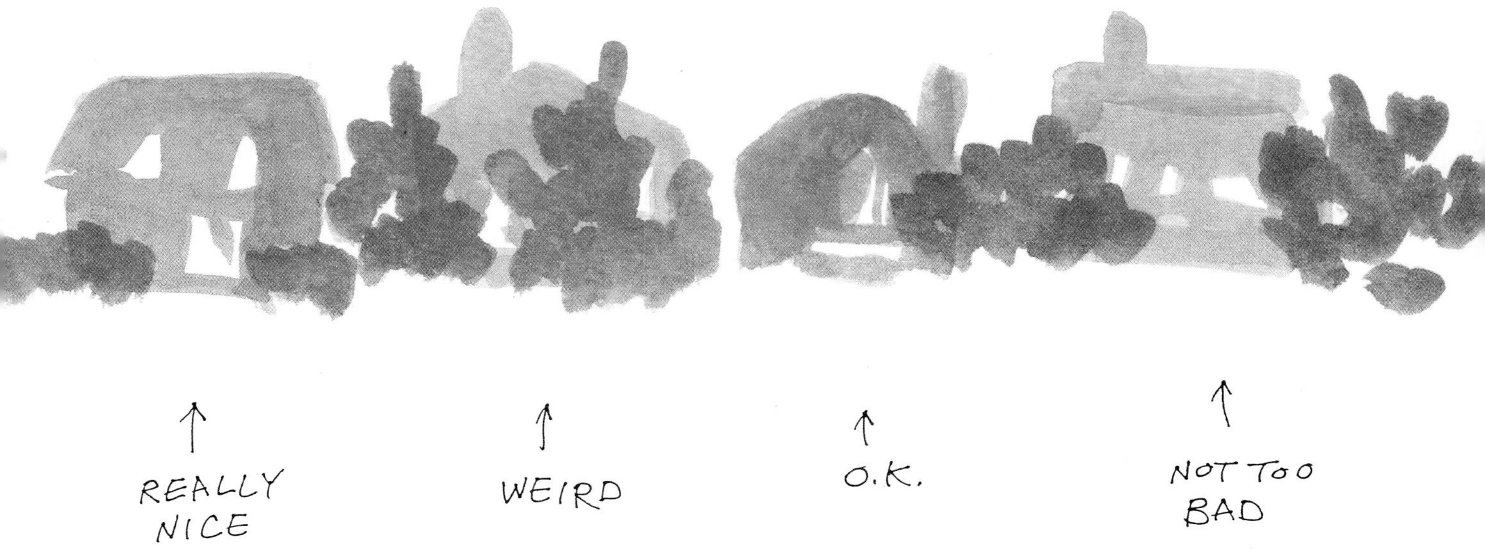

↑
REALLY
NICE

↑
WEIRD

↑
O.K.

↑
NOT TOO
BAD

On the wall of the post office in the village
were pictures of criminals nobody could find.
There was a big reward if you found them, so . . .

THERE! LOOK!
THAT'S ONE OF
THEM!

NO, IT ISN'T.
THAT'S THE
GARBAGEMAN!

my brother and I kept our eye out.

There were a lot of things I couldn't do.

I couldn't make
a loud whistle
with two fingers.

I couldn't learn to juggle.

But I could wiggle my ears

one at a time.

And I could fall over on my face without getting hurt.
(You put your hands up at the very last minute.)

Across the street were woods.
In the summer there were vines to swing on.

In the winter we built
forts and threw snowballs.

We made tunnels in the snow.

If it wasn't snowing or raining, my brother
and I walked to school. Jocko watched us.

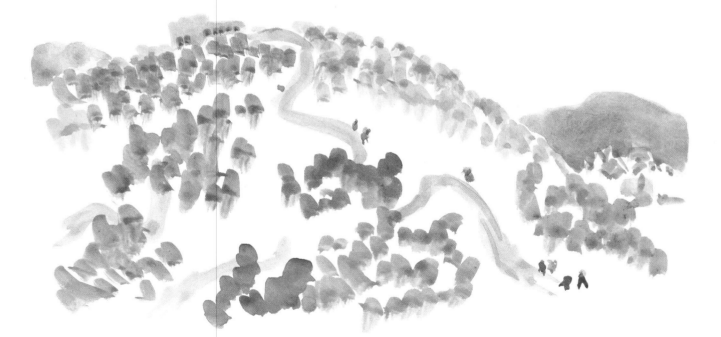

The village had steep hills and twisty roads.
Other children joined us on the way to school.

I liked making things
with clay
in art class.

You took a fat hunk of it

and rolled it into a long piece

and curled it around

and put it on top
of another long, curled
piece, and another.

Then you smoothed it
all out and painted it
and baked it—

and took it home
to your mother.

IT'S FOR
YOU.

OH, HOW
LOVELY!

Sometimes it was hard for me
to pay attention in school.

What was on the
blackboard was never
as interesting

as what was out the window.

And Davey Gronowski was always making me laugh.

My brother liked to scare me.

He said I was a scaredy-cat and afraid of everything.
That wasn't true. . . .

The only things I was afraid of were:

BEES

HOSPITALS

BATS

THE DENTIST

SNAKES

TOUGH KIDS

IODINE ON CUTS

TICKS ON JOCKO

THE BULL THAT
LIVED IN THE
MEADOW DOWN
THE ROAD

THE DARK

LIGHTNING

I was also afraid of the dam breaking.
Sometimes we went for a picnic at a big dam.
My brother would suddenly say, "I think the
dam is breaking," and I would start to run.

The worst thing that happened was
when Jocko got hit by a car.

No bones were broken, but he was hurt.

HERE'S SOME
WATER, JOCKO

HERE'S A BONE

Jocko stayed very quiet for a few days
and then he got well again.

My brother kept a diary.
He wrote in it every day.
I begged him to let me see it.

PLEASE CAN
I SEE YOUR DIARY?

NO! IT'S
SECRET!

PLEASE?

OH, COME ON!

PLE-E-E-ZE?

NO!

NO!

NO!!

One day, when he was away,
I took his diary down
from the shelf . . .
and I read it.

Every day was the same!

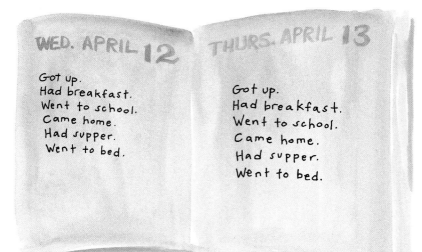

WED. APRIL 12

Got up.
Had breakfast.
Went to school.
Came home.
Had supper.
Went to bed.

THURS. APRIL 13

Got up.
Had breakfast.
Went to school.
Came home.
Had supper.
Went to bed.

I put it back on the shelf.

Sometimes our family would take the train to New York City.
The railroad station was at the edge of the river.
You had to go over an overpass to get to the track.

GO
RIGHT
→

While you were waiting, you could watch
fast trains coming with thick smoke and
cinders flying from their smokestacks.
At the last minute . . .

you'd run for safety!

When the train for New York arrived,
we'd climb aboard.

My father was used to going on the train, so he read
the newspaper. The seats were shiny woven wicker.
If it was hot, you could open the window and get
the breeze.
There was plenty to see.

In New York we once went to the
top of the Empire State Building.

I CAN SEE OUR HOUSE!

NO, YOU
CAN'T!

We always had lunch at the Automat.
The food was behind small glass windows.
When you saw just what you wanted, you
put money in a slot, turned a knob, opened
the window, and took it out.

The most exciting time in New York was when we went to see
our grandparents sail away on a big ocean liner. A band played,
and everybody waved and threw confetti.
When the ship's whistle blew, the whole city seemed to shake.

Tugboats pushed the ocean liner
down the river toward the sea.
I wished I could go.

On the way home I asked,
"Can I go on an ocean liner?"
"When you get older," my parents said. . . .

I couldn't wait to get
higher on the door.